MY FIRST 5 MINUTES FAIRY TALES

THUMBELINA

Wonder House

Once, there was a sweet old woman who lived all alone on a hilltop. She had no family. She wished she could have a baby girl but she was too old.

One day, a kind fairy heard her wish. "Plant this seed in your garden and you shall get a baby girl," she said. The old woman carefully planted the seed.

She took great care of the plant until a lovely flower bloomed from it. There was a pretty, tiny girl inside it! The old woman was delighted. "You are the size of my thumb, so I will call you Thumbelina," she said.

Little Thumbelina had a bed made of walnuts and used flower petals as blankets. She was greatly loved by the old woman.

Croaaaaak!

One day, a giant toad saw Thumbelina and fell in love with her. While she was asleep, he picked her up and carried her to his pond.

He placed her on a lily pad and said in a mean voice, "You can't escape now! I will be back soon."

Thumbelina was terrified! She tried to be friends
with the fishes but even they were mean to her!

A kind swallow saw Thumbelina weeping and felt sad for her.

The swallow spoke gently, "Don't cry, little girl. Climb on my back, I will take you to a safe place."

Thumbelina climbed on the swallow's back
and they soared high in the air.

The swallow took Thumbelina to a garden full of flowers. He said, "Choose any flower you wish as your home, dear one."

Thumbelina stepped inside a sunflower and was approached by a handsome fairy.

"I am the Prince of Flowers," he said. "You are welcome to our kingdom!"

Soon, the fairy Prince and Thumbelina
fell in love. They got married and lived
happily ever after amongst the flowers!